Out-of-this-world Events

KELL and the
DETECTIVES

THE ALIENS, INC. SERIES

KELL and the DETECTIVES

By Darcy
Pattison

pictures by
Rich Davis

MIMS HOUSE / LITTLE ROCK, AR

Mims House
1309 Broadway
Little Rock, AR 72202

www.mimshouse.com.com

Publisher's Note: This is a work of fiction. Names, characters, places, and incidents are a product of the author's imagination. Locales and public names are sometimes used for atmospheric purposes. Any resemblance to actual people, living or dead, or to businesses, companies, events, institutions, or locales is completely coincidental.

Book design © 2013 by BookDesignTemplates.com

Pattison, Darcy. 1954-

p.cm.

Summary: When the school principal discovers that aliens have zigzag fingerprints, she thinks she'll finally track down the aliens at her school.

Kell and the Detectives/by Darcy Pattison

Series: Aliens, Inc. 4

Hardcover ISBN: 978-1-62944-028-6

Paperback ISBN: 978-1-62944-029-3

eBook ISBN: 978-1-62944-030-9

1. Aliens-Juvenile fiction 2. Schools- Juvenile fiction 3. Mystery-Juvenile fiction I. Pattison, Darcy II. Kell and the Detectives III. Aliens, Inc Series, Book 4

Library of Congress Control Number: 2014918924

Lexile 510L

Printed in the United States of America

CHAPTER

My hands dripped with blue paint. On my paper, I finger painted a straight blue line.

Beside me, my best friend Bree swept a finger through red paint.

Mrs. Crux, the art teacher, had shown us a graffiti cartoon called, "Kilroy Was Here." It was a funny bald man looking over a wall.

KiLROY was here

"Use finger paint to draw something looking over a wall," she said. Each table had paper plates with finger paint and rolls of paper towels.

"What are we going to do for you-know-who's birthday party?" Bree whispered.

She smeared a fat red line on her paper, and then, a bald head.

"Shh. You-know-who is right there." I nodded toward the table next to us where Aja was drawing bald men, too.

Maybe I would draw a bald girl. Or a bald elephant. Or maybe I would draw my Dad hiding behind a wall and write, "An alien was here."

My family owns Aliens, Inc., and we do birthday parties for Earthing kids. Aja Dalal's mom asked us to do a surprise birthday party for Aja. Because he's a good friend, it's hard not to tell him about the party. It has to be a surprise, though, or Aliens, Inc. won't get paid. But without asking Aja, I didn't know what kind of party to plan.

The classroom door opened, and Mrs. Lynx, the principal, walked in.

"Mrs. Lynx, I am painting bald aliens," Aja called. "Would you like to see?"

Mrs. Lynx stepped over the Aja's table and studied his finger painting of an alien. Everyone knew that Mrs. Lynx was the president of the Society of Aliens Chasers, the S.A.C. She only wanted one thing, to catch an alien.

And here's the truth, the whole truth and nothing but the truth. I, Kell Smith, am an alien from the planet of Bix. I worry that some day Mrs. Lynx will catch me and sell me to the government.

"The eyes are wrong," she said. "Aliens have silver eyes."

I rolled my silvery eyes at Bree and she shrugged.

"Yes," Aja said. "But they don't make silver finger paint."

"Oh, of course. Well, it's good except for the eyes." Mrs. Lynx nodded to him. She walked around looking at paintings thumbtacked to bulletin boards.

An
Alien SPY
Was here

Mrs. Lynx stopped in front of a painting of a sky with three suns. She bent closer, and then spun around to stare at the art class. Her voice got excited. "Whose painting is this? You forgot to sign your name."

I sank down low in my chair. That was my painting of my home planet, Bix.

Mrs. Crux said, "Those aren't signed because they are just practice pieces."

"But look!" Mrs. Lynx pointed to my picture. "The fingerprints."

Aja jumped up and ran to look. "Oh!"

"What?" My voice shook, but no one noticed because they all crowded around my painting.

Aja's eyes were big. "Human fingerprints have circles. This fingerprint has zigzags. There's an alien in our class."

I stared at my hand and fingertips. I didn't know that Bixsters had different fingerprints from Earthlings. I was going to be caught. I shivered in fear.

Mrs. Crux waved at the paintings. "These are from all my classes yesterday, mate. I don't know who did that painting. It could be from any grade."

That was lucky for me. Bree and I shared an art desk, so she knew it was my painting. But she was the only one who knew.

Aja got up close to the painting and pointed his purple finger at one spot. "Maybe the painter used a pencil point to draw a zigzag on the fingerprint. I wish I had my magnifying glass."

Mrs. Lynx said, "Yes! If I had my magnifying glass, we could be detectives. We would figure this out."

Aja's dark eyes were bright with excitement. "Do all aliens have the same fingerprint? Or does each alien have a different fingerprint, like humans?"

Mrs. Lynx nodded. "Those are good detective questions."

"I want to be a detective and solve crimes," Aja said. "The hardest thing is learning to observe. You have to see what is there, not what you expect to see there."

"It's the same with chasing aliens," Mrs. Lynx said. "If you expect to see a person, you see a person. I never expect to just see a person. I always know that there might be an alien around."

Bree pulled me back to a table away from the other kids and whispered, "I know what kind of party to do for Aja. A detective party."

"How do you do a detective party?"

"We'll need detective hats," Bree said quietly. "They call them Deerstalker hats."

It was time for a Detective Party Look Up Later List:

1. What is a detective?
2. What is a deerstalker hat?"

Mrs. Lynx tapped my Three Suns Over Bix painting, again. "This is my lucky day. I'm going to catch an alien. Class, hold up your hands for me to look at your fingertips."

Bree's back got stiff and straight. She marched up to Mrs. Lynx. "No, ma'am." She sounded just like her Mom, who is a lawyer. "You can't look at my hands without my parent's permission."

Mrs. Crux nodded. "She's right, mate."

Bree had just saved me!

Mrs. Lynx frowned.

The bell rang.

"I have to watch the hallways. Mrs. Crux, please save that painting." Mrs. Lynx pointed to a bulletin board and said. "Put it over there, so I know where it is."

Without waiting for an answer, she stomped out to monitor the hallways between classes.

Kids ran back to their tables to clean up and go to the next class.

Mrs. Crux took my Three Suns painting and thumb tacked it to the Accidental Art Bulletin Board. I had 19 other paintings on that Bulletin Board. What if some of those accidentally had my zigzag fingerprints, too? I had signed those paintings and Mrs. Lynx would catch me.

I had two choices. I could destroy all my paintings, even the ones on the Accidental

Art Bulletin Board. Or I could put alien fingerprints on lots of paintings.

"Freddy," I said. "I'll put up your wet painting."

I carried paintings for Freddy, Aja, Mary Lee, Bree, and a couple other kids. When I put up a wet painting in a shelf, I also touched a couple others. When someone looked the next day, most of the paintings would have zigzag fingerprints.

That should confuse Mrs. Lynx and the S.A C.

Finally, I went to the sink and washed my hands. Bree was washing finger paint off her hands, too. "Are you OK?"

I dried my hands and stuck them in my armpits to hide the fingerprints. "No."

"We'll think of something," she said.

What did she know? Earthling girls have soft hands and circle fingerprints.

CHAPTER

2

I hid my hands in my pockets all day. After school, Bree and I met on the school playground to walk home. The playground was right beside the street. A new concrete fence blocked out noises from cars, and that was good. But it was painted all white, and that was a very long, very boring fence.

At home, I hurried to the kitchen for a snack. Mom and Dad sat at the table drinking coffee with Doc East. When Mom cooked, the kitchen often smelled like burned toast. Now, it almost smelled like dovitch, which is a Bixster drink. That was impossible, though, because the replicator was still broken.

I looked from Doc East to Mom to Dad. My stomach flip-flopped. Something was going on. Doc East is our family doctor. Mom got sick last month, an allergic reaction to a bee sting. Doc East saved her life. He's a human doctor, but he is learning to be a doctor for Bix aliens.

"Mom, what's wrong? Why is Doc East here?"

We gave away the beehives, but I worried every day that she might be allergic to something else on Earth.

"Nothing is wrong." Mom's silver eyes lit up. "In fact—"

"What's that yummy smell?" Bree had followed me inside. She's a friend, but she does say funny things like "yummy."

Dad said, "I fixed the replicator. I just made Doc East a cup of dovitch." He sipped his own cup and looked happy with himself. Back on Bix, Dad is an astro-physicist. Here on Earth, he is a party planner. And he fixes things.

"Why is the Doc here?" I asked.

"We have a surprise for you," Mom said.

Bree said, "May I try some dovitch?"

I frowned. Bree didn't like grawlies, my favorite Bix food. I didn't think she would like dovitch, either.

"I'll make you a cup," Dad said. He put white cubes in a coffee cup and stuck it in the replicator.

"What are the white cubes?" I asked. We had used up all the replicator's starting cubes that we brought from Bix. Dad experimented with lots of different things. Everything he tried stank up the kitchen and didn't work. Maybe he finally found something to use. I just hoped it was cheap, and it was easy to get.

"I used sugar cubes," Dad said. "They worked."

I knew what I was going to have for supper, grawlies!

"Did you hear me?" Mom said. "We have a surprise."

"OK," I said. "But first show me your hands."

an ant was here

I turned her hands over to look at her fingertips.

Bree leaned over to see, too. "The same as yours."

I held up her hand for Doc East to look. He studies the differences in animals, and he is very interested in how aliens are different from humans.

He looked but shrugged.

Bree said, "It's like Aja said. People see what they expect to see." She sipped from her cup and said in surprise, "This dovitch is pretty good." She spooned in more sugar and took another sip.

I said, "Dad, look at your fingertips, and then, look at Doc East's fingertips."

Doc East held out his hand. He's the tallest Earthling I have ever seen. In college, he played basketball. His hands were so big, he could hold a basketball with just his palms, no fingertips.

Dad, Doc East and Mom all compared fingertips.

Dad said in surprise, "Circles."

Doc East said in surprise, "Zigzags."

"Yes! What are we going to do?" I explained about finger paint, and how I added alien fingerprints to a lot of the pictures in art class.

"Leave it to me," Dad said. "I'll think of something."

Mom crossed her arms. "Now, will you listen to my surprise?"

I nodded.

"No," Mom said. "I'll show you my surprise."

She led us out to the greenhouse. My mom is a botanist on Bix, which means she loves plants. The greenhouse stays warm even in the winter. She grows both Earthling and Bixster plants.

"Look," she said.

Hidden in the corner of the greenhouse was a red leather cushion. The center was dented. Balanced in the dent lay a soft green, egg-shaped thing. I looked closer. No, it wasn't egg-shaped. It was an egg.

Mom had laid an egg! Wow!

My Mom had laid an egg. A green egg. An egg!

No wonder Doc East was here. No wonder Mom and Dad were grinning.

"Is that a plastic dinosaur egg?" Bree asked. Earthling girls see what they expect to see. "No," I said. "I'm going to have a brother."

.

CHAPTER 3

The next morning in Social Studies class, Mr. Martinez's bald head gleamed in the morning sun. He looked like a real live Kilroy-was-here.

Mr. Martinez
was here

Next to him stood Mrs. Crux, the art teacher.

I groaned. This was going to be another project where two teachers worked together. Those were always hard projects.

Mr. Martinez said, "How do you study history?"

We all looked at each other. Was this a trick question?

Bree raised her hand and said, "You study history by reading the history book."

Mr. Martinez nodded. "Yes. What I should have said is, how do historians study history?"

We all looked at each other again. This was a very strange question.

I raised my hand and said, "They look at old things and read old books and old documents. I guess they like anything old."

"Yes," Mr. Martinez nodded.

But that wasn't the answer he wanted. He waited.

No one said anything.

Mrs. Crux said, "Historians are almost like detectives. They study clues and made conclusions about the clues."

"Historians are detectives?" Aja frowned.

Mrs. Crux and Mr. Martinez unrolled a huge piece of paper and taped it to the wall. It was a colorful mess of crazy art. One section had food wrappers taped down. Another section had lots of words.

"This is a piece of graffiti," Mrs. Crux said. She explained that graffiti is painting or writing on the side of a building, sidewalk, fence, or in some public place. Kilroy-was-here was graffiti when it was drawn in a public place. If you write on the bathroom walls, that's graffiti. Usually, you get in trouble for making graffiti, and Mrs. Crux reminded us we better not draw on school walls. "This time," Mrs. Crux said, "I asked some teachers and staff to make graffiti posters."

"Who made that poster?" Aja asked.

"That's what you have to figure out." Mr. Martinez beamed. "You must make observations about the graffiti poster. Next, you will guess who made it. That's what historians do. They look at pieces of pottery or old letters. Then they guess how ancient people lived. And then they look for more clues to see if they guessed right or not."

Mrs. Crux held up four more rolls of paper. "If you guess correctly, there will be prizes on Graffiti Day."

"Prizes!" yelled Freddy. "I love prizes."

I groaned, "Graffiti Day?"

Mrs. Crux's beamed. "Graffiti Day has two parts. For the history part of Graffiti Day, you guess who made one of these posters. Remember, each poster was done by someone on the school's staff. For the art part of Graffiti Day, we will be painting graffiti on the new schoolyard wall."

That was a great idea. That long white wall needed color.

"What kind of graffiti will we paint?" Bree sounded excited.

"You have to do drawings and have your design approved," Mrs. Crux said. "But beyond that, it's up to you."

Just one more thing worried me about Graffiti Day. "Do we have to work with someone else or just do it alone?"

"Team work!" said Mrs. Crux and Mr. Martinez together.

Mrs. Crux said, "You'll do your own art project. But to figure out the graffiti posters, you'll work in a team."

The whole class slumped in our seats. Graffiti Day had sounded fun, but it was too good to be true. Teamwork was always hard.

Mrs. Crux said, "Each team will be given one poster to figure out."

My group was just boys: Roman, Freddy, and Aja. Bree got Mary Lee, Ting, and Kailee—all girls. We would show those Earthling girls!

Mrs. Crux said, "Teams can take turns coming up and looking closely at the graffiti poster. Be sure to take notes on what you observe."

"We need a list," I said.

Teachers at Our School
Principal: Mrs. Lynx
Art: Mrs. Crux
Music: Mr. Vega
Language Arts: Mrs. Tarries
Health/Nutrition: Mrs. McGreen
Science: Mrs. Parrot
Social Studies: Mr. Martinez
Math: Mrs. Sand
P.E.: Mrs. Tan

When it was our turn to study our graffiti poster, I made another list.

Things on the Graffiti Poster
Torn piece of oatmeal box
Wrapper from a diet drink
White socks
Three peacock feathers
Map of Mexico

We stared at each other. Who would make a graffiti like that?

Freddy said, "It has to be a woman. Those are women's socks."

But Roman said, "Maybe. But what if they are from someone's wife?"

"Who likes diet drinks?" I asked.

That was a clue we could work with. We just needed to watch teachers at lunchtime. Or watch them when they went in and out of the teacher's room. Or, maybe look in their trashcans. We could find someone with a diet drink, I was sure.

The graffiti words were not in English. I copied some of them down. Later, I would look them up on the Internet.

We talked about each graffiti clue and decided that we needed to observe the teachers better. The Graffiti Day contest was hard! But the boys team would beat the girls team.

At home, I dropped my book bag on the kitchen table. I grabbed a snack and went out to the greenhouse. I sat cross-legged and talked to my brother, the Green Egg. I told him all about crazy Earthling schools and about Graffiti Day.

"If someone looked at things in our house," I said, "they would know we are aliens. We live on Earth now, but we are still Bixsters."

The greenhouse door opened and shut. Dad sat cross-legged beside me and asked, "Have you been out here long?"

I shrugged. "I'm just talking to Greenie Boy. Will we give him a Bixster name or an Earthling name?"

"Both," Dad said.

"Did you know that there are lots of words for green in English? I could call him Greenie Boy, Avocado Boy, Forest Green Boy, Lime Boy, or Jade Boy. Those are all synonyms for the word green." I ran a finger down the side of my brother's egg. "Dad, will we ever go home to Bix?"

GREENS

moss · · · · · · · · · · avocado

Spring OLIVE ～～～～

CELADON

Dad sighed. "We are still trying to call home, but it doesn't work. We might be here a long time."

I blinked, because my eyes were suddenly full of tears. Avocado Boy would hatch on Earth, not on Bix where he should be. I couldn't change that. But I didn't have to like it. I didn't mind this Earth adventure. It was interesting. And fun. But a baby should hatch at home, not in a strange place. I blinked hard.

I changed the subject. Changing the subject is when you talk about something else so you don't have to talk about what worries you.

"I don't like Jade Boy out here all alone," I said. "What if something happens? Can we set up a video camera?"

"Great idea!" Dad jumped right up. Maybe he needed that change of subject, too.

We went right then and bought a video camera. We hooked it up to the Internet and my cell phone, Mom's cell phone and Dad's cell phone.

Now, I could watch Emerald Boy any time I wanted. And while I was at school, Mom or Dad could watch him.

When I showed Bree the Egg Cam, the video of Evergreen Boy, she asked, "How do you know it's a boy?"

That surprised me, but it shouldn't. How on Earth would she know anything about Bixster eggs? "Green eggs are always boys. Yellow eggs are always girls."

"Not pink?"

"Ugh. Pink eggs would be ugly," I said.

"If I was hatched from an egg, I would want a pink egg," Bree said.

Earthling girls like pink WAY too much.

CHAPTER

4

One day the next week, Dad handed me a box of fake fingerprints. It was two weeks before Graffiti Day and Aja's surprise birthday party. Each fake fingerprint was a strip of plastic with zigzags on it. You peel off the back,and it has sticky stuff. Stick it to your finger, and you have instant alien fingerprints.

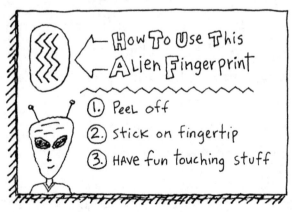

Dad said, "Put these where kids will find them. Don't let anyone see you do it, though." He explained that if everyone wore fake fingerprints, someone would get caught.

"You want them to get caught wearing fake fingerprints?" I said.

"Yes. Mrs. Lynx will think that all the alien fingerprints are fake. Just some kids playing around," he said.

Dad even had small cards that explained how to use the fake fingerprints.

I put some of the fake fingerprints and cards in the boy's bathroom. Bree put them in the girl's bathroom. We left some in the art room by the sink.

"Did anyone see you?" Bree asked.

"No one," I said. "We're too sneaky."

Later in art class, I scribbled on my paper in frustration. What graffiti art could I do for the playground wall? Not a picture of the Bix sky with three suns.

I picked up a color and just started drawing. A minute later, I was looking at Olive Green Boy.

Mrs. Crux passed by and said, "Nice, mate. It looks like an Emu egg. Emus live in

Australia, you know. They look like an ostrich. Their eggs are big and dark green."

That was funny. Greenie Boy looks like an Emu egg. I said, "I"ll draw some more."

"Good idea," she said.

I drew and drew and drew green eggs, until I had a drawing full of eggs. Mrs. Crux liked it and said to color it.

Before I started with color, though, I took a short break. I got up to look at other student's art. Some were using finger paints, and I saw a couple kids using fake fingerprints. Our plan was working. Most kids had the plastic strips only on their index fingers. But Aja wore one on each finger.

Grinning, I sat back down and used watercolor paints for my eggs. I was never going to use finger paints again.

When I finished, Mrs. Crux said, "It's a good design. You can paint it on the playground fence on Graffiti Day."

In between classes, I checked the Egg Cam. Lime Boy was still where we had left him.

Later in social studies class, the graffiti detective teams met. We tried to answer the questions about our graffiti poster:

Who likes diet drinks?
Who wears white socks?
Who likes traveling to Mexico?
What do peacock feathers mean?

Aja, who wanted more than anything to be a detective, had news. "I know who likes diet drinks. Mrs. Tarries and Mrs. McGreen."

Mrs. McGreen taught health and nutrition, so that made sense.

But Freddy had other news. "Mr. Vega has on white socks today."

"No," I said. "He has on boots. You can't see his socks."

Freddy said, "Right before class started, he took off his boot and scratched his foot. Then he put the boot back on. I saw it myself. White socks."

Roman said, "I know what language those words are written in. Spanish. It says, 'Someday, I will go home again.'"

Earthling languages are strange. I thought that in Mexico, they would speak Mexican. Instead, in Mexico, they speak Spanish. Mr. Martinez grew up in Honduras, and they speak Spanish there, too. But there was a map of Mexico on the poster, not Honduras. Did Mr. Martinez ever live in Mexico?

"What about the oatmeal and peacock clues?" I asked.

But no one in our group had an answer.

I updated the list of teachers with what we knew.

Updated List of Teachers

Mrs. Lynx, principal – Former science teacher.

Mrs. Crux, art – From Australia. Knows about emus, not peacocks.

Mr. Vega, music – White socks. Likes to eat peanut butter.

Mrs. Tarries, language arts – African American, diet drinks, likes microwave popcorn.

Mrs. McGreen, health/nutrition – diet drinks, eats carrots for snacks

Mrs. Parrot, science – Likes orange drinks

Mr. Martinez, social studies – From Honduras, where they speak Spanish. Only drinks coffee.

Mrs. Sand, math – Never eats or drinks in her classroom.

Mrs. Tan, P.E. – Asian American. Likes French fries almost as much as Aja.

In the quiet, we heard Bree say, "Good, I think we have it figured out."

My head jerked up. The girls were all smiling. They knew who made their graffiti poster.

My team groaned. We had to do some good detective work before Graffiti Day or the girls would win.

After history, I checked the Egg Cam again. Mom was sitting beside The Egg on a huge pillow. It was her new stomach pillow. But it was hot to wear, so at home, she just sat on it.

The next day in art class, Mrs. Lynx walked in with in a magnifying glass as big as a dinner plate. She had done this a couple times already, but she kept coming back to make new observations. Again, she studied every painting on the Accidental Art bulletin board. This time, she copied the zigzag fingerprints into a small notebook.

Bree and I watched and frowned.

Aja watched from his table and frowned. He stood up once, but sat back down. In the end, though, a detective  hates for another detective to be wrong. He marched over to Mrs. Lynx and handed her a fake fingerprint and the instruction card.

Great! That's exactly what Dad wanted to happen.

Mrs. Lynx read the card. She put an alien fingerprint on her index finger. She dipped it in paint and then touched my picture of the Three Suns of Bix. It made a new alien fingerprint.

Mrs. Lynx didn't yell.

Mrs. Lynx didn't get mad.

Instead, she smiled. "Aja," she said, "those aliens have tricked you. You think all the fingerprints are fake. You're wrong. These fake fingerprints prove that there are aliens. Think. When did you see these fake fingerprints for the first time?"

"This week," Aja said.

"Right," Mrs. Lynx said. "After I found the first zigzag fingerprint."

"Oh," Aja said.

"Yes," Mrs. Lynx said. "After. That means the aliens are trying to fake us out."

"You are a good detective," Aja said.

"Thanks." Mrs. Lynx pulled off the fake fingerprint, and stuck it to the back of the instruction card. "These are good clues," she said. "I will go analyze them." She picked up her magnifying glass and walked out.

Bree whispered, "What now?"

I sat on my hands. "I need to wear gloves from now on."

"No, you need fake Earthling fingerprints," she said.

"Hey! That might work," I said. "I just can't let Mrs. Lynx see my hands."

Bree said, "See my thumb?"

I stared at it.

"Gee, you're dumb," Bree said, and then laughed to show me it was a joke.

I didn't laugh. I don't understand Earthling jokes.

CHAPTER 5

B ree and I kept talking about Aja's surprise party. It was hard to plan a party for someone when you can't ask them what they will like. You have to observe them and try to figure them out.

One day at lunch, Aja did his French fry trick.

"Watch," he said. "This time I'll break a record."

Freddy laughed, "My record is 30 fries at a time. You can't break that."

We counted out loud while Aja stuffed all his French fries into his mouth. –14, 15. And then, he stuffed all of Bree's French fries into his mouth. –27, 28, 29.

He waved at my fries, and his eyebrows went up in a question.

I nodded.

—30, 31.

Freddy frowned and said, "You have to eat them now. No fair if you spit them out. It doesn't count until you've eaten them all."

Aja just nodded and started chewing. He chewed. And chewed. And chewed.

Meanwhile, Freddy told a chewing joke: "What's the difference between a train and a teacher?"

When no one could answer, Freddy said, "A teacher says 'spit out your gum' while a train says, 'CHEW CHEW!'"

I laughed, but I didn't really get it. Earthling jokes are hard to understand.

By the end of lunch, Aja had chewed up and swallowed all 31 French fries.

Aja was the French Fry King!

On the way to the next class, Bree said, "For Aja's party, we need a French Fry table. There will be plain fries, spicy fries, cheesy fries, curly fries, and sweet potato fries."

I agreed. But that still left cake. Maybe Mom could ask Mrs. Dalal about Aja's favorite cake flavor.

After school, Mom took Bree and me to the costume shop. I was ready for a surprise when I opened the door because Mr. Jasper always has on a funny mask. But this time, Mr. Jasper wasn't there. Instead, behind the counter, I saw a man with a big black mustache, a long black beard, black bushy eyebrows, and thick black glasses.

"Hello, Mr. Jasper," Mom said.

I looked all around for the shop owner, but I only saw the bearded man.

The bearded man said, "Good afternoon, Mrs. Smith. What can I help you with today?"

It was Mr. Jasper! Instead of a mask, he wore fake hair on his face! He reached up and smoothed down the mustache. He had fooled me again.

Mr. Jasper said, "Mrs. Smith, are you expecting?"

Mom blinked at Mr. Jasper. "Expecting? Expecting what?"

He looked at her stomach. "Expecting a baby?"

Mom patted the pillow under her shirt. When Moss-Green Boy hatched, people needed to think he had just been born. Which meant that Mom had to look pregnant like an Earthling mother.

"Yes," Mom said. "Soon we'll have a baby."

"When's it due?"

Bree said, "In a couple weeks."

"Really? You don't look big enough," Mr. Jasper said.

Mom looked scared.

That pillow stomach looked HUGE to me. How big was it supposed to be?

But Bree knew what to say. "She's just skinny and doesn't show much."

"Right. Well, good luck with the new baby, Mrs. Smith. What can I help you with today?"

Mom explained that we were doing a detective party.

"You'll want Deerstalker hats, of course," Mr. Jasper said. "Also, I have a special piñata that might interest you."

Bree laughed and clapped her hands. "I love piñatas."

PIÑATAS

Mr. Jasper led us to a room with colorful piñatas hanging from the ceiling. Bree explained to me that they held candy. To use it, you blindfold a kid and give him or her a heavy stick. The kid tries to smash the piñata with the stick. When someone finally breaks open the piñata, it spills out candy.

"Yummy," Bree said.

I rolled my eyes.

Mr. Jasper pointed to a black piñata that was covered with red question marks. "When this one breaks open, there's no candy. Only detective clues to follow to find the candy."

"Oh! That sounds like fun," Bree said.

"Where will you do the party?" Mr. Jasper asked.

Bree and I looked at each other. We had forgotten to ask Where. We knew Who, What, When, and How. But not Where.

Mom answered, "We'll do it in our back yard."

"Good choice," Mr. Jasper said.

"Any other suggestions for games?" Mom asked.

Mr. Jasper pulled at his fake beard. It came off in his hand! "No," he said. "Deerstalker hats and piñatas are good. Maybe you should read detective stories for party ideas."

At home, Bree followed me to the greenhouse to talk to Jade Boy. We told him all about the detective party. I asked him, "What other games can we play?"

Avocado Boy didn't answer. I wondered if he would look like Mom or Dad. Or maybe he would look like one of my grandparents. I stopped thinking about that, though, because it made my eyes fill up with tears again.

"Bree, you can talk to Forest Green Boy, if you want."

She tilted her head and looked at me. Her forehead wrinkled like she was worried. I thought she might ask me about the tears. Instead, she said, ""No. I want to sing to him."

That Bree, she sings as sweetly as Bix crooners, the royal birds. When she sings, it makes the sun come out and shine inside me. And the tears go away.

This time, she sang a funny, happy song called, "The Hokey Pokey." She made me stand up and do motions with her, too.

You put your right leg in,
You put your right leg out;
You put your right leg in,
And you shake it all about.
You do the hokey pokey,
And you turn yourself around.
That's what it's all about!

Then she sang it again, but instead of right leg, she said, "left leg." When she repeated it again, she changed to a new body part. These are the body parts she sang about: right leg, left leg, right arm, left arm, and head. And then came the last lines.

You put your whole self in,
You put your whole self out,
You put your whole self in,
And you shake it all about.
You do the hokey pokey,
And you turn yourself around.
That's what it's all about!

We collapsed on the floor of the greenhouse and laughed together.

"I'm glad you're smiling now," she said. Without waiting for an answer, she continued, "I'm thirsty. Let's get some milk."

"Yummy," I said.

That made Bree laugh even more. Sometimes, when Earthling girls laugh and sing it makes Bixster tears go away. And that's a sunshine thing.

CHAPTER

It was ten days before Aja's surprise birthday party.

The doorbell rang. I put down my social studies book and clattered down the stairs. Mom was out in the greenhouse, and Dad was gone.

I opened the door.

Mrs. Lynx nodded to me. "Your family is still new in town. I hadn't heard of a baby shower, so I thought I'd just stop by."

What was a baby shower? After they were born, did Earthlings give their babies a public bath or shower?

I asked Mrs. Lynx to wait in the living room.

"Mom!" I burst into the greenhouse, and explained about Mrs. Lynx.

Mom brushed off her dirty hands, stuffed her pillow under her shirt, and waddled into the house. She told me, "Get some tea to serve."

"Thank you for coming by," Mom said. "How can I help you?"

"I came about the new baby," Mrs. Lynx said.

I set down a tray with a pitcher of tea and three glasses.

Mom reached over to hold my hand. Tight. "What about the baby?" Mom's voice quivered in fear.

Mrs. Lynx handed Mom a package wrapped with blue ribbons.

Mom turned loose of my hand and took it. She turned it over and over, unsure what to do.

"Go on," Mrs. Lynx said. "Open it."

"Of course," Mom said. "Would you pour the iced tea, please?"

Mrs. Lynx poured tea into each glass. Carefully, Mom untied each ribbon, folded it, and put it beside her on the couch. To delay opening the box, Mom took a drink of tea, then set her glass down.

Mrs. Lynx stared at Mom's glass. She whispered, "Is that your fingerprint?"

There it was. A dirty zigzag fingerprint.

Mom said, "I've been out in the greenhouse planting things."

"And trying out the fake fingerprints for Aja's surprise party. Right, Mom?" I said.

Mom looked from me to Mrs. Lynx. She nodded.

I asked, "What do you think, Mrs. Lynx? Good joke or not?"

Softly, Mrs. Lynx asked, "May I see your fingertips?"

Mom put her hands behind her back. "My hands are dirty from the greenhouse."

Mrs. Lynx held out her own hand and repeated, "Your hands, please?"

Just then, Dad came in.

While Dad shook Mrs. Lynx's hands, I used my t-shirt to wipe Mom's fingerprint off the glass. At the same time, Mom looked down at the gift box. She pulled up a piece of scotch tape. Deliberately, she put her finger on it, and then pulled it off.

Mom held up the tape. "Look! Zigzag fingerprints! Whoever wrapped this must be an alien!"

Mrs. Lynx blushed and shook her head. "I wrapped that. I'm not an alien."

"Are you sure?" Mom stared at her until Mrs. Lynx looked away.

I took a sip of tea to hide my smile. Mom was smart.

Mom put the tape onto the table. She opened the box, and there was a hand-made quilt. At the top were the letters: S-M-I-T-H.

"You made this?" Mom asked in surprise.

"Yes, I like to quilt," Mrs. Lynx said. "I try to give baby quilts when a family has a new baby."

Mom's face softened. She leaned toward Mrs. Lynx, and I was afraid Mom might try to hug my principal.

"Thank you," Mom said. "We don't have lots of friends here yet, so this is—" Mom stroked the soft quilt. "Thank you."

Dad repeated, "Thank you."

Now there was an awkward silence.

Mrs. Lynx frowned at the scotch tape fingerprint. She opened her mouth to say something else.

Mom did the only thing she could. She grabbed her stomach pillow and moaned.

"Oh! Are you having the baby?" Mrs. Lynx stood abruptly.

Mom moaned and said, "John, would you call Doc East, please?"

Dad took the hint. "Mrs. Lynx, if you don't mind. I think you should come back and visit another time. My wife isn't feeling well."

"Babies are exciting, aren't they?" Mrs. Lynx said. "Maybe this one will come early."

Later, when I cleaned up the tea glasses, I realized that the scotch tape was gone. Mrs. Lynx had taken it. She had my Mom's fingerprint. Now, she had three sets of alien fingerprints: mine, my mom's, and the fake ones. What would the S.A.C. do with them?

This wasn't over. Mrs. Lynx, the president of the S.A.C., suspected my Mom was an alien. Mrs. Lynx wouldn't quit until she had her alien, and had sold it to the government. When Greenie Boy hatched, would his mother still be here? I worried and worried.

After supper Bree came over, and I showed her the SMITH baby quilt. I told her about Mrs. Lynx stealing Mom's fingerprints.

"I'm worried," Bree said.

"Me, too." Somehow, I felt better because Bree was worried, too.

We took the SMITH quilt out to show Greenie Boy.

In the greenhouse, we wrapped the quilt around the egg.

Bree said, "I think I'll sing to him again."

Here's what she sang:

Skinny Marinky

Skinny marinky rinky dinky
Skinny marinky doo
I love you
Skinny marinky rinky dinky
Skinny marinky doo
I love you
I love you in the morning and in the afternoon
I love you in the evening and beneath the silver moon
Skinny marinky rinky dinky
Skinny marinky doo
I love you
I really mean it
I love you
Let's say it again now
I love you

That was a nonsense song. I know this because I asked Bree what it meant.

"Nothing," she said. "It's just fun to say. Try it."

"Marinky."

"Hey," Bree said. "That's what you should name him. Marinky."

I tried it out. "Marinky Smith and Kell Smith." It did sound good. "I'll tell Mom and Dad about that name and see what they think."

"Great," Bree said. "I gotta go now."

Bree opened the door to the greenhouse to leave. But she turned back around and hit me on the shoulder. Wait. Why do Earthling girls do that? Does that mean she likes me, or doesn't like me

CHAPTER

One week before the surprise detective party, Bree and I handed out invitations. It said:

TOP SECRET
 Your mission,
should you choose to accept it,
is to help celebrate Aja Dalal's
birthday.
 It's a surprise,
so don't tell him about it.

The invitations had two giant fingerprints, one human and one fake alien. I wanted to use my real fingerprint, but Dad wouldn't let me.

We passed out invitations on the bus, in homeroom, and at recess, until every kid in third grade was invited. Except Aja.

Aja is a detective.

Aja noticed.

At lunch, Aja plopped down his food tray and slumped onto the bench. "Hey, did any of you get an invitation to a party?"

"What party?" I asked.

"Some one is doing a birthday party next Friday. Is Aliens, Inc. doing a party? What's going on?" Aja said.

nobody Likes me

I looked at Bree. She hates when people lie. Her mother is a lawyer, and she believes you should tell the truth, the whole truth, and nothing but the truth. All the time. But we had to tell a lie! Aja couldn't know about his birthday party because it was a surprise.

"What makes you think Aliens, Inc. might be doing a party?"

"I hear kids talking," Aja said. "But when I come up, they stop talking."

Bree said, "Yes, there's a party."

Aja said, "Am I invited?"

"No," Bree said.

"Oh," Aja nibbled at a French fry. He dropped it onto his plate. "Whose party is it?"

Aja looked so sad that I wanted to tell him. But I couldn't. "Does it matter?"

"Don't worry." Aja lifted his chin and looked grim. "I'm a detective. I'll figure out why I'm not invited."

Bree opened her mouth, but I frowned and shook my head.

Aja stood and carried his food tray to the trashcan. He dumped it all out—even his

French fries. He never lets anyone throw away French fries. He was upset.

Aja shoved open the cafeteria doors and went out to the playground by himself.

Bree said, "Can't we tell him?"

"Mrs. Dalal was very clear. If Aja finds out about the party, she won't pay Aliens, Inc.," I said. "And my family needs that money."

To change the subject, Bree nodded to my cell phone. "Can I see the Egg Cam?"

We looked at Greenie Boy. Nothing had changed. He was pretty boring.

I told Bree, "I know Aja is upset, but I'll figure out something."

"Good," Bree said. "You're great at figuring out things."

All that week, we worked on Graffiti Day. During art class, we went outside to the playground wall. Mrs. Crux showed us the third-grade section, and we drew out our designs. By the end of the week, drawings filled the wall. From twenty feet away, the drawings were hard to see. That was OK. Everything was ready for Graffiti Day when we would put color on that boring wall.

At night, Bree and I worked on Aja's party.

"Do we have to have cake?" I asked.

"No. It is tradition, but we don't have to," Bree said. "Did your mom find out what kind of cake Aja likes?"

"His mom says that he likes sugar cookies, not cake."

"Then let's do sugar cookies shaped like mustaches," Bree said. "And ice cream. And that's enough."

It was good to have that decided. The Surprise Detective party planning was going well. We had food and games and almost everything figured out. Except Aja was sad,

sad, sad. His feelings were hurt because he thought everyone was invited to a party except him.

Aja, one of my best friends, was hurting. And I had to let him hurt.

Maybe Earthlings shouldn't do surprise parties.

CHAPTER

G raffiti Day dawned clear and warm. It would be a good day for painting the white wall around the playground. I put on some old jeans and a torn up shirt. They were good paint clothes, and it wouldn't matter if I paint on them.

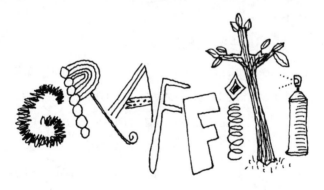

Before I left for school, I stopped in the greenhouse to check on Greenie Boy. Mom said that he would hatch any day now.

All was quiet. I checked the Egg Cam, and it was working.

Each class had an assigned time to paint. Third grade was right after lunch. We'd be the last class to paint the wall. And then, we'd have the Graffiti Day assembly. Freddy wanted to win a prize for guessing who did our graffiti poster. But the Boys Team was going to lose to the Girls Team. We still didn't know who did our poster.

It was a long, slow morning. Finally after lunch, it was time for us to paint. We raced out to the wall.

Except Aja. He walked.

For the past week, he had walked everywhere with a frown on his face. And I hadn't told him anything about his surprise party. I felt like I was a bad friend.

 Mrs. Crux and some parent volunteers had set up long tables beside the wall. Each table had one color of paint on it. The

green table had five different greens. The red table had seven cans of colors. I asked for a cup of avocado green and smeared the color onto the largest egg in my drawing. Olive green went onto the smallest egg. In between, I painted moss green, spring green, and celadon green.

Mrs. Crux came by and said, "Great job. The Emu eggs are wonderful."

"Thanks," I said.

I walked back to the paint table, and just as I got there, I tripped.

My cup of green paint flew up and up and up. And then, it came down and down and down. Right onto Aja's dark hair.

Aja turned slowly. He scowled. He was mad.

He grabbed two cups of red paint and charged. He knocked me over and sat on top of me and poured paint onto my face.

Coughing, spluttering, I shoved him off.

Someone yelled, "Paint fight!"

Around us, kids starting grabbing paint cups and throwing at each other. They slapped paint brushes at each other. Paint splattered everywhere.

But Aja and I just stood and glared at each other.

I shrugged. "It's a surprise party. For you."

"What?" Aja's dark eyes went wide with shock.

"Your mom hired Aliens, Inc. to give you a surprise party."

"You mean everyone is invited—"

I finished it for him. "—to your party."

"Oh." Emotions flitted across his face. Relief. Anger. Surprise. Joy.

"Yes. Oh."

He shook his head. "But why didn't you tell me?"

"It was supposed to be a surprise," I said. "Now, your mom won't pay Aliens, Inc. Because I told you."

Freddy and Mary Lee ran by covered in orange paint. Bree had a swipe of red paint down the back of her t-shirt.

"I'm sorry," Aja said. "I just thought—"

"—that no one liked you. Wrong. Everyone is coming, and everyone is excited."

Aja frowned. "Can I just act surprised tomorrow?"

"You are a good detective. Are you a good actor?" I asked.

"Yes!" Aja yelled.

There was a sudden quiet.

The paint fight around us had stopped and everyone turned to look at Aja. He just started laughing, and I laughed with him. It was good to have my friend back. Besides he looked silly with green paint dripping from his eyebrows.

Mrs. Crux set up hoses for kids to wash off. It was a good thing that kids had worn painting clothes today.

We went in and out of the school building, and the glass door got filthy. In fact, it had lots of my zigzag fingerprints on the door. I decided to clean them off. I went to the Sanitation Room and knocked.

"Hello?" Mr. Chamale opened the door. He grinned. "You have a green stripe in your hair."

I grinned back at him. "You should see the other kids."

He nodded and turned to get his mop and bucket.

I said, "If you give me supplies, I'll try to clean off the glass doors."

"Thanks for the help." He picked up a basket, put glass-cleaning supplies into it, and handed it to me. But I was looking around the Sanitation Room.

An old battered desk stood in the corner. On the desk was a vase. And in the vase were a dozen peacock feathers.

"Why do you have those?" I asked.

Mr. Chamale ran a hand along a feather. "Back in Mexico, my parents had a peacock farm. We had a couple peacocks, the males with big tails. We also had a large flock of pea hens, the females. That meant we always had lots of pea chicks. My father sold the peacock feathers and did quite well."

Oh, that Mrs. Crux. She was tricky. Mr. Chamale wasn't a teacher, but he was on the staff at the school. I tried to remember exactly what she said: "I asked some teachers and staff to make graffiti posters."

You see what you expect to see. You hear what you expect to hear.

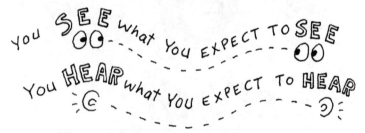

I asked Mr. Chamale, "Do you like diet drinks?"

He held up a diet Coke.

"Can I see your socks?" I asked.

He pulled up his pants leg. White socks.

"Are those women's socks?" I asked.

 Mr. Chamale shrugged. "I have small feet and women's socks fit better. What difference does it make?"

"It's your graffiti poster!"

"You guessed it. I wanted something abut my life in Mexico. I'm an immigrant—an alien from another country."

English is a strange language. I'm an alien because I'm from another planet. Mr. Chamale is an alien because he's from a different country.

Mrs. Crux is an immigrant and alien, too, because she's from Australia. If she did a graffiti poster, it might have pictures of kangaroos. Or sheep, because she was raised on a sheep farm in Australia.

Why did it take the Boys Team so long to figure this out? I wondered: Do kids really see or hear the adults in their lives?

Quickly, I ran upstairs and cleaned my fingerprints off the glass doors.

The bell rang. Time for the Graffiti Day assembly.

At the front of the cafeteria, the graffiti posters sat on easels. One by one, teams guessed who made each poster. Bree's all-girl team correctly guessed that Mr. Vega, the music teacher had done their poster. That was too easy. Only his poster had written music.

Finally, it was my team's turn to guess who did the peacock-feathers poster.

"Mr. Chamale," I said.

"Correct," Mrs. Crux said.

Aja slapped my back and said, "You're a good detective."

"Thanks," I said.

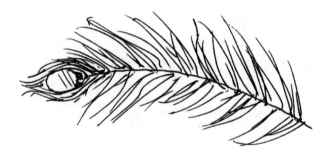

On the way home, Bree asked how I figured out the peacock feathers belonged to Mr. Chamale.

"Fingerprints," I said. And then I explained about cleaning off the glass doors.

Bree said, "That makes sense. Detectives always figures out things from fingerprints."

"I have a surprise for you," I said. Mr. Chamale had given me a small peacock feather, and I gave it to Bree.

"Oh! It's beautiful," she said. And that smile from an Earthling girl must have lit up a galaxy.

.

CHAPTER 9

The day of Aja's surprise birthday party, we worked all day. It was hard for Mom, because people were around all day. That meant she had to wear her stomach pillow the whole day. She was hot and tired.

Plus, she checked the Egg Cam every few minutes. We didn't want people to see us walking into and out of the greenhouse all day.

"I know it will be today," Mom said. "When you hatched, I told your grandparents all day that it was

The Day. They didn't believe me, but I just knew. And I know that today is The Day for Greenie Boy."

Dad just patted her stomach pillow and said, "Jane, we have work to do."

And she went off to help him rake the back yard, decorate tables, and make sugar cookies.

At 6 p.m., kids started to arrive. They sat in our living room, waiting for Aja to arrive.

Thirty minutes later, a van pulled up outside our house. Everyone stood in the dark room and waited. I checked the Egg Cam again, but someone hissed at me, "Get that light out."

I turned off the phone and stuck it in my pocket. Nothing was happening anyway. Mom was wrong. This wasn't The Day.

Outside, we heard Mrs. Dalal call, "Aja, help me with this box."

A few moments later, the doorbell rang. Mom answered it and Aja stepped into the house.

I flipped on the light and we yelled, "Surprise!"

Startled, Aja dropped the box. "What?"

We yelled, "Happy birthday!"

Aja looked at his mom and dad. "Did you do this?"

Mrs. Dalal nodded and waited, hoping that he would be pleased.

"Wow!" Aja hugged his mom, and then his Dad. "Thanks. I thought you had both forgotten about my birthday."

I almost cried at how touching the scene was. Until I rememberd that Aja already knew about the party. He was a good actor!

Secretly, I gave him a thumbs up, and he grinned back.

And then, the fun began. Kids walked out the front door and around to the side yard. I opened the fence and let them in one at a time.

Our backyard was transformed into a crime scene. To come in, kids had to duck under yellow and black tape that said, "Crime Scene: Do Not Enter."

Everyone who walked in was a suspect. First, they had to stop at the fingerprint table.

Doc East asked, "Do you want a real fingerprint or an alien fingerprint?'

Once they chose, he rolled their fingers— with or without the fake fingerprints—on an ink pad and then on a piece of paper. Everything was put in their Police File to take home.

Then, party-goers dressed like detectives. At the next table, they got a deerstalker hat and a magnifying glass. On each name tag, Mrs. Crux drew a line, and then drew the person's face. Underneath, she wrote, "Freddy was here." Or, "Bree was here."

Next, the party-goers became victims. Mom worked the Dead Man Photos. When a person is murdered, sometimes the police draw chalk lines around them. The body is taken away, but the police can still see where the body had lain. So, on our wooden deck, we drew chalk lines. One by one, kids laid down in the chalk lines and

Mom snapped their picture. The photos would be in the kid's Police File to take home.

Bree's mom, Mrs. Hendricks, was dressed in robes like a judge. She glared at each kid. Then she used a wooden hammer called a gavel, and banged it on the table. She yelled, "Off to jail!"

That was OK. Jail just meant the refreshments table.

Aja stopped at the French fry table and stared. "I am in heaven," he said.

Dad was in charge of the ketchup bottle. "No food fights tonight, please," he said.

It was great detective party, except two things. Mrs. Lynx, the alien detective, walked around, eating sweet potato fries, and watching everything.

Dad squirted ketchup on her plate and asked, "Are you having a good time?"

Mrs. Lynx said, "Of course. I am a detective who finds aliens."

And that was very bad because the second problem was Greenie Boy. His egg was rocking. Not much. I found Mom and showed her the Egg Cam

Mom said, "Not now! He has to wait a couple hours."

"Babies don't know how to wait," I said.

"Keep an eye on it. When the crack is halfway across the egg, let me know," she said. "I'll think of something."

Suddenly, I realized that Mrs. Lynx was right behind me. She was looking over my shoulder at the Egg Cam.

Quickly, I turned it off, but the Earthling Alien Detective had already seen my brother starting to hatch.

Aliens were here

CHAPTER

Mrs. Lynx took my phone out of my hands. "What was that? Something is hatching. What is it?" She turned on the phone and stared.

Mrs. Crux joined us and said, "Show me." Mrs. Lynx turned the phone around to show Mrs. Crux the Egg Cam.

She looked up at me. "That's an emu egg. Right? Like your graffiti painting."

What on Earth did Mrs. Crux or Mrs. Lynx know about Bixster eggs? Nothing. We had to bluff them. "Oh, yes," I said. "It's an emu egg."

"Where's it from, mate?" Mrs. Crux asked. "A zoo or something?"

That made me mad. My brother wasn't something from a zoo.

Bree was calm, though. She said, "An emu farm in Australia has this cool Egg Cam."

Mrs. Lynx tapped the picture on the phone. "Emu egg? Are they really a deep green like that?"

I held my breath. Would she believe it?

Mrs. Crux nodded. "Oh, yes. An Egg Cam is just the sort of publicity an emu farm might do."

"Nice egg." Mrs. Lynx handed me back the phone and wandered back to the French fry table.

I wanted to run to the greenhouse and watch my brother hatch. Instead, we played party games.

Kids had been fingerprinted as suspects, given detective badges, had their pictures taken as victims lying in a chalk mark, and been sent to jail. Now was the best part: kids would get to be real detectives.

It was time for the piñata.

Aja whacked it open on the first try.

Surprise! Only pieces of paper fell out.

Aja picked up one and read, "To find the candy, follow these clues."

Dad called, "You are a team of detectives! Work together to find the candy."

Aja read out the first clue. "Look in the biggest tree house."

Mr. Martinez stood beside a ladder and helped Freddy climb up to the tree house. Freddy stuck his head out and called, "Clue #2: Look under the refreshments table."

Quickly, Mary Lee crawled under the table and came out with a piece of paper. "This was taped underneath there," she said. "Clue #3: Ask the judge for a clue."

I snuck my phone out of my pocket and checked the Egg Cam. The egg was cracked on top!

Mario was close to the judge's table. He asked, "Your Honor, do you have a clue for us?"

Mrs. Hendricks pounded the gavel on the table and said, "Clue #4: Look at the Crime Scene tapes."

Now, everyone ran around looking at the yellow Crime Scene tape. It just said "Crime Scene." Until, Mario and Roman yelled together, "Look!"

Ardy
was here

One section of Crime Scene tape had other words written in black marker.

Aja laughed. "You see what you expect to see. We expected to see the words 'Crime Scene' so we didn't see anything else."

The Egg Cam showed that the crack was now a tiny hole. I looked all around at the party. Suddenly tears filled my eyes. I was one lucky alien to have so many friends. Maybe, if I had to stay here on Earth for the rest of my life, it wouldn't be so bad. Maybe it would be a good place for Greenie Boy, too.

Roman called out, "Clue #5: Look under the French Fry table."

Aja pushed up the table cloth. "Look!" He pulled out a box with small paper bags.

Each bag said, "Detective Pay Day."

Dad explained, "As payment for all your hard work, each detective will take home a bag of gold coins."

Aja laughed. "I love chocolate coins."

"Aja, come blow out your candles!" Dad said.

Mom had made a chocolate cupcake, just for candles. We sang and Aja blew out his nine candles. Then everyone ate mustache sugar cookies and drank poison. Of course, it was just black colored punch, not real poison.

We watched Aja open his presents. He had three detective books, a chemistry set, and a poster that showed famous detectives.

I walked around the outside of the circle of kids and showed Mom the Egg Cam.

Bree said, "I'll go and watch him. No one will miss me."

Mom shook her head. "It's cracked all the way around. We need to be in there now."

She grabbed her pillow stomach and groaned.

Mrs. Lynx said, "Oh! Is the baby coming? Too bad, because I haven't caught my alien yet." She sighed. "Next time. I have three fingerprints and fingerprints almost always solve mysteries. It's just a matter of time."

At that, Mom looked pale and scared. She said, "Doc East, what should we do?"

Quickly, Doc East sent the kids home. Each kid-detective took home a bag of chocolate coins, a couple mustache cookies, and their own Police files.

"Do you need us to drive you to the hospital?" Mrs. Lynx asked.

"No," Mrs. Hendricks said. "She's going to have a natural birth here at home. Doc East is here so everything should be fine. We just need some privacy now." She walked Mrs. Lynx to the back-yard gate and waved good-bye.

Aja, his mom, and his dad were the last to go. "Thank you, Mr. Smith," said Mrs. Dalal. "This was a great party. I'll send you a check tomorrow."

"Thank you," Dad said. "We're just glad that Aja was surprised."

I sighed in relief. Mrs. Dalal had never figured out that Aja knew about the party.

Finally, the Dalals left.

We were alone. And we ran to the greenhouse.

Greenie Boy had broken a small hole in the egg.

Mom didn't help. "He has to do this himself," she said.

He rested. Then, small fingers reached out and ripped away the top of the egg.

Marinky Smith was here. He was bald. And he squalled. How could something that small make that much noise?

Mom pulled my brother out of his egg.

Doc East was snapping pictures and the Egg Cam was recording everything.

Marinky put his arms around my Mom's neck and clung there. She made crooning noises and he calmed down. Mom had the SMITH baby quilt ready, and she wrapped him up in it.

First, my Dad held him and crooned to him in Bix, telling him, "You're a fine son."

And it hit me. My brother was both an alien and an Earthling. What kind of a life would he have?

And then, it was my turn. I sat cross-legged on the greenhouse floor, and Mom put Marinky in my arms.

He was small, with silvery eyes like mine. He had a small chin like Mom, but the rest of his face looked like Dad.

I smiled at every Earthling and alien around me. "It's my brother."

Bree's eyes were glowing with excitement. She shook her head and said softly, "Alien boys are weird."

This time, it didn't make me mad, because I knew what she meant: "Brothers are amazing."

I looked down and Marinky Smith smiled at me.

And right there in the middle of the greenhouse, in the northern hemisphere of the planet Earth, in the Sol system, in the Milky Way galaxy, the Earthling sun came out and shone in my heart.   And it still surprises me when it does that.

THE END

The stars
were here

FOR FUN

HIDDEN SOMEWHERE WITHIN THE PAGES OF THIS BOOK ARE "KILROY" DRAWINGS OF MR. MARTINEZ, KILROY, HUMPTY DUMPTY, JR., AN ANT, STARS, ARDY, AN ALIEN, AN ALIEN SPY, AND FREDDY. CAN YOU FIND ALL OF THEM?

The Answers are at MimsHouse.com/aliens

Kell's Teachers

Mrs. Lynx   Mrs. Sand   Mrs. Tarries

Mr. Martinez   Mrs. Parrot   Mrs. McGreen

Mrs. Crux   Mrs. Tan   Mr. Vega

ALIENS INC. EGGLESS CAKE RECIPE

Remember this conversation between Kell and his Dad in Book 1?

I nodded, then said, "I have to tell you about school today. First, I have to tell you something else--Earthlings are born, not hatched."
"I know."
"And you didn't tell me?"

Kell was outraged when he found out that humans weren't hatched from eggs and Dad hadn't mentioned that fact. But things got even worse, when Kell found out that Earthlings eat eggs.

To put on a birthday party, Aliens, Inc. had to serve cake. But Kell refused to make cake with eggs.

A BIT OF EGGLESS CAKE HISTORY

In the U.S., Eggless Cakes were common during World War II, when many foods were rationed. My first eggless, milkless, butterless cake was just such a vintage recipe. There are multiple versions, but all involve boiling up a sugar syrup, then adding flour. Most recipes are for a single 8" or 9" cake, probably because WWII also saw flour rationed and people just made small cakes. When you take away eggs, milk and butter, though, you must give the cake something to make it taste good! Adjust the spices to your own taste. Some recipes only use cinnamon, and some double the raisins. Personally, I regularly substitute craisins for raisins in lots of recipes. Kell agrees with me!

KELL'S EGGLESS CAKE

1 cup white sugar
2 tablespoons shortening
2 teaspoons ground cinnamon
1/2 teaspoon ground nutmeg
1/2 teaspoon ground allspice
1/2 teaspoon salt
2 cups craisins (dried cranberries)
1 1/2 cups water
1 teaspoon baking soda
2 cups all-purpose flour
1 teaspoon baking powder

Directions

Preheat oven to 350 degrees F (175 degrees C). Lightly grease one 8" or 9" square cake pan.

In a saucepan over medium high heat combine; the sugar, shortening, ground cinnamon, ground nutmeg, ground allspice, salt, raisins, and water bring to a boil and continue boiling for 5 minutes. Remove from heat and let cool.

Sift the flour, baking powder and baking soda together. Add the flour mixture to the cooled craisin mixture. Stir until just combined. Pour batter into prepared pan.

Bake at 350 degrees F (175 degrees C) for 20 minutes.

Enjoy this Aliens, Inc. style Eggless Cake! But please—no cake fights!

ALIENS, INC. SERIES: BOOK 1
KELL, THE ALIEN

Shipwrecked on earth and desperate to make money, an alien family decides to make a living by opening Aliens, Inc., an intergalactic event-planning business master-minded by 9 year old alien boy, Kell Smith.

Kell discovers that his neighbor, Bree Hendricks, turns 9-years-old next month and she wants a party with an alien theme. That should be simple as flying from star to star. But things aren't that easy: Earthling's ideas about aliens are totally wrong. Even worse, Principal Lynx is a UFO-Chaser and suspects aliens around every corner.

Will the Aliens totally blow the Aliens Party? Will Principal Lynx capture Kell and his family and them over to the government?

ALIENS, INC. SERIES: BOOK 2
KELL AND THE HORSE APPLE PARADE

Kell, Bree, and the Alien, Inc. gang return to plan a new event, a Friends of Police parade. But Principal Lynx believes someone in third grade is an alien, and she scans each student with her new Alien Catcher App. Kell and Bree deal with 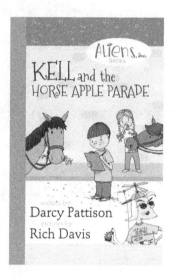 City Hall, figure out fund-raising, and keep the Parade marching. When the Society of Alien Chasers (S.A.C.) attends the Parade, Kell must find a way to keep his family safe. Join the fun-loving aliens from planet Bix for another out-of-this world adventure

ALIENS, INC. SERIES: BOOK 3

KELL AND THE GIANTS

Fun and Humor: Giants Stomp Through this Story!

If you're an alien on Earth, you have one giant secret to keep. After a while, even friends want to tell your secret. Kell and Bree plan a birthday party with giants—Big Foot, Cyclops, Goliath and the Jolly Green Giant— while they struggle with keeping their own giant secret. But they have an even bigger problem: Principal Lynx and the Society of Alien Chasers is back with a dog trained to sniff out an alien in a crowd. When Mom is stung by a bee, Kell must find a doctor who can keep a giant secret, too. Will Aliens, Inc. be able to pull off the Giant Party and keep everyone happy?

DISCOVER WHAT OTHER READERS ALREADY KNOW:

"Amusing, accessible, engaging" – Publisher's Weekly review of Aliens, Inc. Chapter Book series, Book 1: Kell the Alien

Art Teachers: Every volume stars with a scene in the art classroom, creating something fun.

Family story: When the Smith family is shipwrecked on Earth, they must learn to depend on each other.

Join our mailing list.

MimsHouse.com/newsletter/

Other Books in
The Aliens, Inc. Series

Book 1: Kell, the Alien
Book 2: Kell and the Horse Apple Parade
Book 3: Kell and the Giants
Book 4: Kell and the Detectives

Other Books by Darcy Pattison

I Want a Dog: My Opinion Essay
I Want a Cat: My Opinion Essay
Saucy and Bubba: A Hansel and Gretel Tale
The Girl, the Gypsy and the Gargoyle
Vagabonds
Abayomi, the Brazilian Puma:
Wisdom, the Midway Albatross:
The Scary Slopes
Prairie Storms
Desert Baths
19 Girls and Me
Searching for Oliver K. Woodman
The Journey of Oliver K. Woodman
The River Dragon

ABOUT THE AUTHOR & ILLUSTRATOR

Translated into eight languages, children's book author **DARCY PATTISON** writes picture books, middle grade novels, and children's nonfiction. Previous titles include *The Journey of Oliver K. Woodman* (Harcourt), *Searching for Oliver K. Woodman* (Harcourt), *The Wayfinder* (Greenwillow), *19 Girls and Me* (Philomel), *Prairie Storms* (Sylvan Dell), *Desert Baths* (Desert Baths), and *Wisdom, the Midway Albatross* (Mims House.) Her work has been recognized by **starred reviews** in *Kirkus*, *BCCB*, and *PW*. *Desert Baths* was named a 2013 Outstanding Science Trade Book and the *Library Media Connection*, Editor's Choice. She is a member of the Society of Children's Bookwriters and Illustrators and the Author's Guild. For more information, see darcypattison.com.

RICH DAVIS, illustrator for the Aliens, Inc series has wondered, "What could be better than getting to do black and white cartoon work for a sci-fi easy reader?" Working on this book has been one big fun-making experience. Rich has also illustrated 12 other children's books, including beginning reader series, *Tiny the Big Dog* (Penguin). His joy is to help kids develop creatively and he has invented a simple drawing game (Pick and Draw.com) and an activities book as a fun tool that now have a following around the world. He frequently does programs at schools and libraries in order to draw with thousands of kids yearly. For him, it is a dream come true and he recognizes that the source is from God alone.

CPSIA information can be obtained
at www.ICGtesting.com
Printed in the USA
LVHW082154150419
614297LV00022B/913/P